Mighty Ants

Exploring an Ant Colony

by Alice Boynton and Wiley Blevins
illustrated by Kathi Ember

RED CHAIR PRESS

Imagine That! books are produced and published by Red Chair Press

Red Chair Press LLC   PO Box 333   South Egremont, MA 01258-0333

www.redchairpress.com

 FREE Lesson Plans from Lerner eSource
and at www.redchairpress.com

Publisher's Cataloging-In-Publication Data
Names: Boynton, Alice Benjamin. | Blevins, Wiley. | Ember, Kathi, illustrator.

Title: Mighty ants : exploring an ant colony / by Alice Boynton and Wiley Blevins ; illustrated by Kathi Ember.

Description: First edition. | South Egremont, MA : Red Chair Press, [2017] | Series: Imagine that! | Interest age level: 006-009. | Includes Fact File data, a glossary and references for additional reading. | Includes bibliographical references and index. | Summary: "The mighty ant has been around since the age of dinosaurs. These hard-working insects can be found on every continent except Antarctica. Readers discover how ants work as a team and why they've been able to survive so long as we explore an ant colony."-- Provided by publisher.

Identifiers: LCCN 2017930463 | ISBN 978-1-63440-274-3 (library hardcover) | ISBN 978-1-63440-276-7 (paperback) | ISBN 978-1-63440-278-1 (ebook)

Subjects: LCSH: Ants--Behavior--Juvenile literature. | Insect societies--Juvenile literature. | CYAC: Ants--Behavior. | Insect societies.

Classification: LCC QL565.2 .B69 2017 (print) | LCC QL565.2 (ebook) | DDC 595.7961782--dc23

Copyright © 2018 Red Chair Press LLC
RED CHAIR PRESS, the RED CHAIR and associated logos are registered trademarks of Red Chair Press LLC.

All rights reserved. No part of this book may be reproduced, stored in an information or retrieval system, or transmitted in any form by any means, electronic, mechanical including photocopying, recording, or otherwise without the prior written permission from the Publisher. For permissions, contact info@redchairpress.com

Technical charts by Joe LeMonnier

Photo credits: Shutterstock, Inc

First Edition by:
Red Chair Press LLC   PO Box 333   South Egremont, MA 01258-0333

Printed in the United States of America

0517 1P CGBF17

Ants are industrious, or hard-working, insects that live mostly in colonies. In a colony, hundreds or thousands of ants live and work together as a team. Sometimes ants even have to solve problems as a team. Worker ants take care of the colony and search for food. Other ants take care of newborn ants. These amazing insects have been around since the time of dinosaurs. They can be found on every continent on Earth, except Antarctica. Are you ready to explore how ants live and work?

Table of Contents

Exploration Begins. 4

Fact File 30

Words to Keep 31

Learn More at the Library 32

Index 32

"Gram, have you seen our ball?"

Soñia and Freddy started looking on every shelf and under every bag.

"*Niños, por favor!*" said Gram. "Please, we need to get ready. You're getting in the way."

"You're like ants at a picnic," Dad said, smiling.
Freddy started crawling around like an ant. Everyone laughed. Everyone except Soñia. She stood still and got a faraway look.

Suddenly, Soñia was standing in tall, tall grass. A wooden table loomed over her like a skyscraper. A foot the length of a football field stood inches away.

Where am I? she wondered. Sniff, sniff. *Barbecue!*

Just then, a chunk of hamburger in a bun came crashing down. An ant dashed straight to it.

"Oh, no! Ants!" thundered a voice.

Sonia laughed. "Now I see what Dad meant."

The ant was hard at work. She cut off a corner of the bun with her sharp jaws and carried it off. "You're a scout searching for food," said Soñia. "Hey, wait! I'll help."

It's a Fact

Ants can lift 5 times their weight; that's like a 50-pound kid lifting a refrigerator. If the food is very large, ants try to break it up. If they can't, they find a way to work together to lift and carry the load.

Soñia pulled at the bun with all her might. She tore off a piece. "Wow, this is heavy," she said. "Ants are tiny, but they are really strong."

Sonia hurried to catch up. The ant kept stopping to rub her **abdomen** on the ground. "She's leaving a trail, so her fellow ants can go back for the rest of that food."

It's a Fact

Ants leave a scent on a trail from food they find. But if something or someone rubs out part of the ant's path, the line of ants stops because they can't smell the trail leading to the food.

Suddenly, Soñia saw a spider ahead. It didn't look very itsy-bitsy to her. Was it seeing its lunch? The spider climbed on a leaf. *Whew, we're safe!* But were they?

The ant kept going. Zig, zag, stop and rub. Zig, zag, stop and rub. Soñia trudged behind her. *Are we there yet?* she thought. They hadn't gone much further when… Danger!

IT'S A FACT

Ants are too small for large predators, but smaller creatures like birds, snakes and spiders do prey on ants. Despite the dangers, ants as a species have survived on Earth for more than 100 million years—from the time of dinosaurs!

A lizard, ready to pounce, spotted them. But then it eyed something bigger—a tasty grasshopper—and off it went.

"Leaping lizards!" said Soñia. "There are so many **predators** here. And we're the **prey**!"

The ant arrived at the **colony** safely. She tapped each ant with her **antennae**. The message: *I found food*. The ants rushed to follow her trail.

IT'S A FACT

The antennae are the most important part of an ant's body. They are used to smell, touch, taste and hear.

Soñia slid down a long tunnel and into the ant nest. *Thud!* As she caught her breath, she looked around.

The tunnels were like hallways. They connected room after room. Hundreds of ants were coming and going.

"Wow, this is an ant city," Soñia said. "I'm going sightseeing."

The first room Soñia peeked into was filled with seeds. Along came some ants with the bun. "The ants store food for when they need it, like we do," Soñia said. "That's so smart!"

Food Storage

IT'S A FACT

Ants have the most advanced brains of all insects. Their higher intelligence helps them overcome most obstacles.

Soñia couldn't wait to see more. She crawled along the tunnel, dodging ants. "Hmm, there's no one directing traffic," she said. "But they all seem to know where to go and what to do."

Soñia stopped. Up ahead, a line of ants dug up dirt, carried it out, and came back for more. Dig, carry, dump. Dig, carry, dump.

IT'S A FACT

To dig out an amount of dirt that would fill a child's sand pail takes 500,000 loads of dirt for ants.

"They're digging a new tunnel," said Soñia. "They're like construction workers. And they don't even have steam shovels to help!"

But the ants had their own special equipment. Their **mandibles**, or jaws, did the job.

Nearby, ants carried out bits of trash. "They're the sanitation workers," said Soñia. "They keep the nest clean."

Every ant had a specific job. *Don't they ever take a break?* Soñia wondered.

Cleaners

IT'S A FACT

Ants even clean themselves; they have a comb on their front legs to remove dirt from their antennae and their bodies.

The next room puzzled Soñia. "What's this?" Ants were tending what looked like tiny fat worms. "Those are larvae," Soñia exclaimed. "This is the ant nursery."

Nursery

IT'S A FACT

It may not seem like it, but ants do sleep! They take naps several times a day. They sleep for a few minutes, then wake up and go back to work.

Nurse ants fed the wiggling larvae. Each wiggle seemed to mean: *More, more, give me more!*

Soñia knew larvae grew from eggs. So where did all the eggs come from?

Soñia found the answer deep inside the nest. She came to a chamber larger and even busier than the others. "Whoa!" she gasped.

There sat the biggest ant Soñia had ever seen. "It's the queen!"

"I get it," said Soñia. "The queen is the *only* ant that lays eggs. She is the mother of all the ants in the colony."

A worker carried each newborn to the nursery. "No wonder the diggers keep making the nest bigger," said Soñia.

Queen's Chamber

IT'S A FACT

A queen Ant can live as many as 15-20 years and may produce millions of offspring.

"Ants are awesome!" Soñia exclaimed.
"I can't wait to tell Freddy."

Soñia scrambled up to the exit. Oh, no! The ant guard blocked the way. *Intruder! Intruder!* Out went the alarm. Ants came running to defend their home.

Just then Soñia heard a far-off voice. "Picnic time!"

Suddenly, Soñia was back in her kitchen. She blinked. What an adventure she'd had!

"We're ready, *niños*," Gram said.

"Freddy and I can help carry stuff," said Soñia. "Teamwork gets the job done."

Then she tucked cookies into her pocket.

"Who are those for?" asked Freddy.

"The ants," said Soñia as she smiled. "They have a lot of mouths to feed!"

Fact File

Stay in Touch Pal! How Ants Communicate

Ants must communicate well to be so successful at working together. They use four senses* to do this.

Smell Ants emit a scent that other ants smell through their antennae. This is how they warn of danger and how they tell of food sources.

Touch Ants tap each other by their antennae to tell about finding food or to ask about food.

Sound If an ant gets trapped in the nest, such as walls collapsing, the ant will wiggle the small joint between waist and abdomen to make a squeaking sound other ants "hear" by vibration through their legs.

Taste Ants may give other ants a sample of food when they return to the colony. They do this by mouth-to-mouth exchange.

* Ants do not have good sight. They depend on their other senses.

Just the Facts!

It's good to be the Queen. The queen ant can live up to 10 or more years. The average life of an ant is only about 50-60 days.

There are 35,000 kinds of ants in the world. Only sixty species of ants are found in North America.

Based on size, if a human could run as fast as an ant, she would run as fast as a racehorse!

How Big?!

The largest ant species in the world is the *Paraponera clavata*. The worker ants can reach a size of 3cm or more than one inch in length! These big ants are found from Honduras to Brazil in rain forests.

shown actual size

Words to Keep

abdomen: the largest part of an ant's body, where its organs and food are kept

antennae: feelers that help ants touch, taste and smell

mandibles: an ant's strong jaws, used to dig, cut and carry things

predator: an animal that naturally hunts another

prey: *(noun)* an animal that is hunted or killed by another for food; *(verb)* to hunt another for food

mandibles

Learn More at the Library

Books

Iasevoli, Brenda. *Ants!* (TIME For Kids Science Scoops). Harper Collins, 2006.

Micucci, Charles. *The Life and Times of the Ant.* Houghton Mifflin Company, 2003.

Whiting, Sue. *All About Ants.* (NG Science Chapters). National Geographic Children's Books, 2006.

Web Sites

Ant Facts for Kids
http://animals.nationalgeographic.com/animals/bugs

BioKids: Ant Facts
http://www.biokids.umich.edu/critters/Formicidae/

CoolKids Facts
http://www.coolkidfacts.com/ant-facts-for-kids/

Index

abdomen	10	predator	13
antennae	14, 21	queen	24-25
larvae	22-23	scout	8
mandibles	20	tunnel	15, 16, 20